THIS OLD MAN

Retold by MEGAN BORGERT-SPANIOL

Illustrated by IRISZ AGOC

CANTATA
LEARNING

MANKATO, MINNESOTA

CANTATA LEARNING

MANKATO, MINNESOTA

Published by Cantata Learning
1710 Roe Crest Drive
North Mankato, MN 56003
www.cantatalearning.com

Library of Congress Control Number: 2014938321
ISBN: 978-1-63290-063-0

This Old Man retold by Megan Borgert-Spaniol
Illustrated by Irisz Agocs

Book design by Tim Palin Creative
Music produced by Wes Schuck
Audio recorded, mixed, and mastered at Two Fish Studios, Mankato, MN

Printed in the United States of America.

VISIT
WWW.CANTATALEARNING.COM/ACCESS-OUR-MUSIC

This old man loves to drum. He can make a **beat** on anything! See what happens as the numbers get higher in this counting and **rhyming** song.

When you hear the dog bark, turn the page.

This old man, he played one.

He played knick-knack on my thumb.

With a knick-knack paddy-whack,
Give a dog a bone,
This old man came rolling home.

This old man, he played two.

He played knick-knack on my shoe.

With a knick-knack paddy-whack,
Give a dog a bone,
This old man came rolling home.

This old man, he played three.

He played knick-knack on my knee.

With a knick-knack paddy-whack,
Give a dog a bone,
This old man came rolling home.

This old man, he played four.

He played knick-knack on my door.

With a knick-knack paddy-whack,
Give a dog a bone,
This old man came rolling home.

14

This old man, he played five.

He played knick-knack on my **beehive**.

With a knick-knack paddy-whack,
Give a dog a bone,
This old man came rolling home.

This old man, he played six.

He played knick-knack on my sticks.

With a knick-knack paddy-whack,
Give a dog a bone,
This old man came rolling home.

17

This old man, he played seven.

He played knick-knack on my best friend.

This old man, he played eight.

He played knick-knack on my gate.

With a knick-knack paddy-whack,
Give a dog a bone,
This old man came rolling home.

This old man, he played nine.

He played knick-knack on my vine.

This old man, he played ten.

He played knick-knack all over again.

With a knick-knack paddy-whack,
Give a dog a bone,
This old man came rolling home.

GLOSSARY

beat—a pattern of sounds made by striking something

beehive—a nest for bees

rhyming—saying words that end in the same sounds

This Old Man

Public Domain

Blue Grass

TO LEARN MORE

Nunn, Daniel. *Counting 1 to 10*. Chicago: Raintree, 2012.

Nunn, Daniel. *Percussion*. Chicago: Heinemann Library, 2012.

Pierce, Terry. *Counting Your Way: Number Nursery Rhymes*. Minneapolis: Picture Window Books, 2007.

Reasoner, Charles. *Hickory, Dickory, Dock*. North Mankato, MN: Picture Window Books, 2014.

Zelinsky, Paul O. *Knick-Knack Paddywhack!* New York: Dutton Children's Books, 2002.